A little caterpillar crawled out of an egg into a big and somewhat unfriendly world. "Where could my mother be," she wondered. Wiggling along a dirt path she observed a worm watching her. "Excuse me, but could you be my mother?" asked the little caterpillar very politely.

Thus began an endearing friendship between a little caterpillar and a worm. Despite their differences, they found much in common and much to share. It was worm who told caterpillar about her next home assuring her that even though they might be apart they would always be friends.

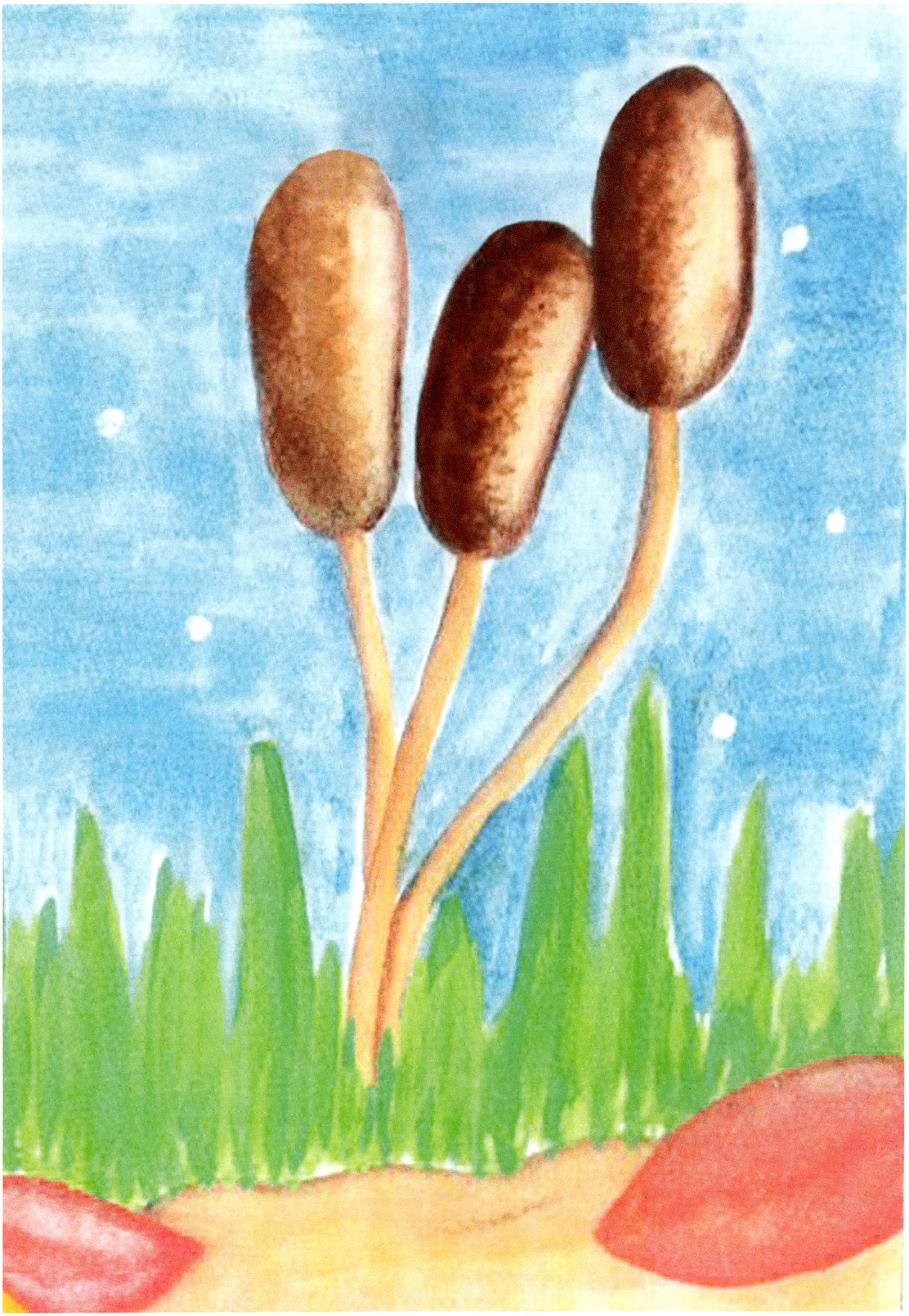

Childhood is joy, trust, pride, kindness, courage, sometimes sadness, but always imagination.

To the children and staff I have worked with and loved at Georgetown Hill Early Schools,

To my family who have contributed so much to my life and to my life's work,

To Melanie Halperin for capturing the endearing personalities of caterpillar, butterfly and of course, wise worm. Thank you.

Wiggle-Dee-Dee

...a story about friendship

By: Ellen S. Cromwell

Illustrated by: Melanie Halperin

Copyright © 2011 by Ellen S. Cromwell. 100329-CROM

ISBN: Softcover 978-1-4628-9458-1
Hardcover 978-1-4628-9459-8

All rights reserved. No part of this book may be
reproduced or transmitted in any form or by any means,
electronic or mechanical, including photocopying,
recording, or by any information storage and retrieval
system, without permission
in writing from the copyright owner.

This is a work of fiction. Names, characters, places
and incidents either are the product of the author's
imagination or are used fictitiously, and any resemblance
to any actual persons, living or dead, events, or locales
is entirely coincidental.

This book was printed in the United States of America.

To order additional copies of this book, contact:
Xlibris Corporation
1-888-795-4274
www.Xlibris.com
Orders@Xlibris.com

In early spring, a little caterpillar crawled out of an egg, stretched her neck, and blinked her eyes in the bright morning sun.

The little caterpillar began looking for her mother. But what did mother look like?

Wiggling along a wooded path, the little caterpillar saw a green grasshopper hiding under a blade of grass. "You are beautiful!" the little caterpillar exclaimed. "Could you be my mother?"

"No," said the polite green grasshopper. "You are looking for something that wiggles…. I hop."

And he hopped away.

After a while, the little caterpillar met a spotted ladybug resting on a lovely leaf. "You are beautiful!" she exclaimed. "Could you be my mother?"

"No," said the gentle ladybug.
"You are looking for something
that wiggles....I fly."

And she flew away.

Nearby, a grey field mouse was making a nest in the middle of a large field. The little caterpillar startled the field mouse. "Excuse me," she asked timidly, "could you be my mother?"

"Me?" responded the unfriendly mouse. "You are looking for something that wiggles. "I run, and if you don't leave immediately,

I will run after you!"

As it happened, the frightened little caterpillar was being observed by a friendly worm. "Please don't be scared," he said. "I won't hurt you."

"Do you wiggle?" asked the little caterpillar.

"I do wiggle," said worm, "but I am not your mother. I can be your friend, if you wish"

"Well, wiggle-dee-dee," said the tired little caterpillar, as she curled up in the worm's dirt home.

Soon after, worm yawned and crawled into his dirt home, while the little caterpillar began to spin her silk home on a milkweed pod near worm's home. Safe and snug, the worm dreamed of digging dirt holes while the little caterpillar dreamed that she was wrapped in beautiful wings, watched over by her mother.

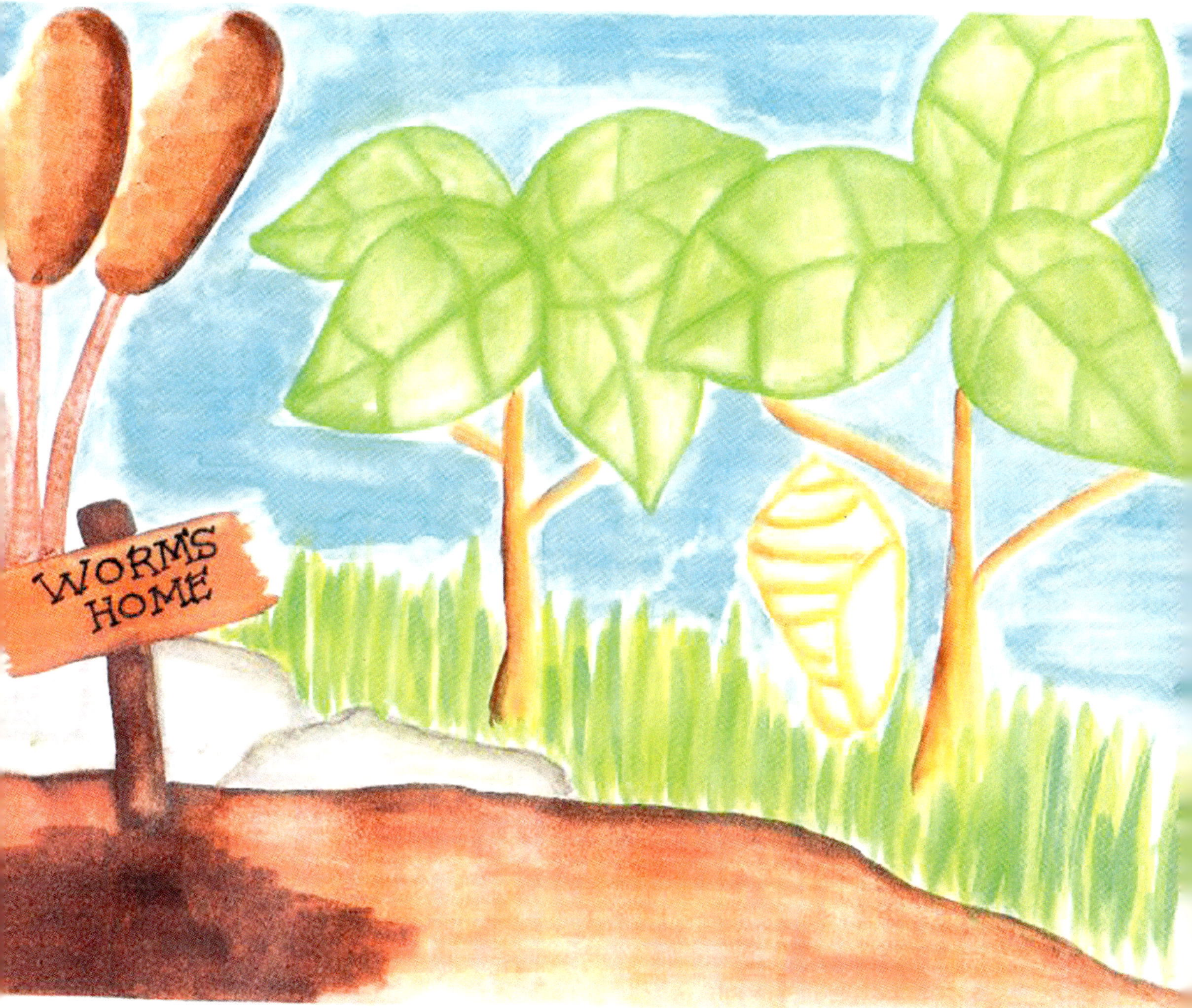
WORM'S
HOME

When little caterpillar awoke, she remembered worm's words.

"You will soon become a butterfly!"

Lifted by the wind, spreading her beautiful wings, she gracefully flew from flower to flower.

In time, the little butterfly grew tired. She could no longer spread her beautiful wings. She only wanted to rest. Remembering her peaceful summer days with worm, she flew back to her favorite resting place- the cabbage leaf near worm's home. It was there that she gently placed her eggs and fell into a deep sleep.

The following spring, a little caterpillar crawled out of an egg that was hidden in a cabbage leaf near worm's home. Blinking her eyes in the morning sun, she crawled past a polite grasshopper, a gentle ladybug, and an unfriendly field mouse. Stopping at worm's home, she said, "Excuse me sir. Could you be my friend?"

"Well, wiggle dee-dee," smiled the wise worm. "I must dig another hole."

Ellen Cromwell is the founder of Georgetown Hill Early Schools In Maryland. Over the years, she has designed curriculum in early childhood development and has written several books on the subject. Her most recent book is "Nurturing Readiness in Early Childhood Education" Allyn & Bacon, 2001.

Melanie Halperin is a Maryland resident, certified in early childhood education, and a long term preschool teacher at Georgetown Hill Early School in Rockville, Maryland. One of her many talents is creating eye catching bulletin boards and wall hangings for little children's enjoyment.

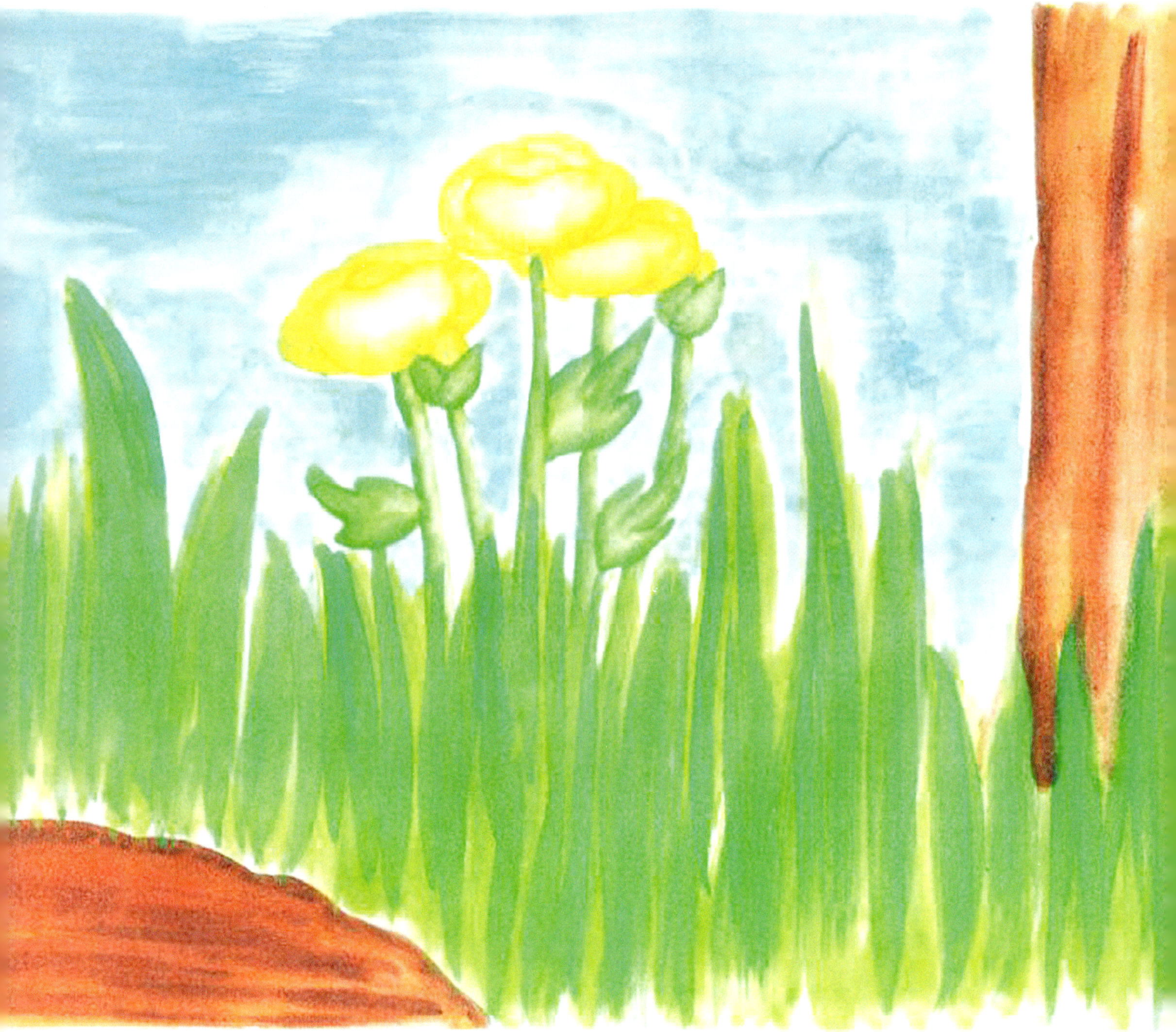